THIS CANDLEWICK BOOK BELONGS TO:

_____

_____

_____

_____

TO THE BEST NANNA IN THE WORLD

WITH LOVE FROM US

First U.S. paperback edition 1996

The Library of Congress has cataloged the hardcover edition as follows :

Murphy, Jill.
A quiet night in / Jill Murphy.—1st.
Summary: Mr. and Mrs. Large's attempt to put the children to bed early and
have a quiet night on their own has an unexpected ending.
ISBN 1-56402-248-X
[1. Elephants—Fiction.   2. Bedtime—Fiction.]   I. Title.
PZ7.M9534Qu   1994
[E]—dc20   93-875

ISBN 1-56402-673-6 (paperback)

2 4 6 8 10 9 7 5 3 1

Printed in Hong Kong

The pictures in this book were done in colored pencil.

Candlewick Press
2067 Massachusetts Avenue
Cambridge, Massachusetts 02140

A Quiet Night In

Jill Murphy

CANDLEWICK PRESS
CAMBRIDGE, MASSACHUSETTS

"I want you all in bed early tonight,"
    said Mrs. Large. "It's Daddy's birthday,
    and we're going to have a quiet night in."
"Can we be there too?" asked Laura.
"No," said Mrs. Large. "It wouldn't be
    quiet with the gang of you all charging
    around like a herd of elephants."
"But we *are* a herd of elephants," said Lester.
"Smarty-pants," said Mrs. Large. "Come on
    now, coats on. It's time for school."

That evening, Mrs. Large had
the children bathed and in their
pajamas before they had even had
their dinner. They were all very cranky.
"It's only four-thirty," said Lester.
"It's not even dark yet."
"It soon will be," said Mrs. Large grimly.

After their baths, the children started
making place cards and decorations for the
dinner table. Then they all cleaned up.
Then Mrs. Large cleaned up again.

Mr. Large arrived home looking very tired.

"We're all going to bed," said Lester.

"So you can be quiet," said Laura.

"Without us," said Luke.

"Shhhh," said the baby.

"Happy birthday," said Mrs. Large. "Come and see the table."

Mr. Large sank heavily into the sofa. "It's lovely, dear," he said, "but do you think we could have our dinner on trays in front of the TV? I'm feeling a little tired."

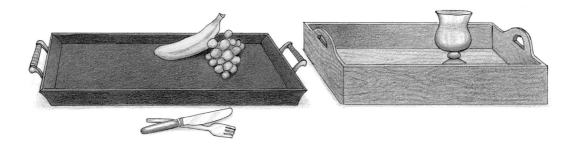

"Of course," said Mrs. Large. "It's *your* birthday.
  You can have whatever you want."
"We'll help," said Luke.
  The children ran to the kitchen and brought two trays.
"I'll set them," said Mrs. Large. "We don't want
  everything ending up on the floor."

"Can we have a story before we
  go to bed?" asked Luke.

"Please," said Lester.

"Go on, Dad," said Laura. "Just one."

"Story!" said the baby.

"Oh, all right," said Mr. Large.

"Just one, then."

  Lester chose a book, and they all
  cuddled up on the sofa.

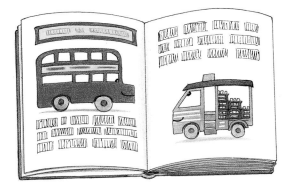

Mr. Large opened the book and began to read:
"One day Binky Bus drove out of the big garage.
'Hello!' he called to his friend, Micky Milktruck—"
"I don't like that one," said Laura. "It's a boy's story."
"Look," said Mr. Large, "if you're going to argue about it,
you can all go straight to bed without *any* story."
So they sat and listened while Mr. Large read to them.

After a while he stopped.

"Go on, Daddy," said Luke.

"What happened after he
   bumped into Garry Garbagetruck?"

"Did they have a fight?" asked Lester.

"Look," said Laura. "Daddy's asleep."

"Shhhh!" said the baby.

Mrs. Large laughed. "Poor Daddy," she said.
"Never mind, we'll let him snooze a little longer
   while I take you all up to bed."
"Will you just finish the story, Mom?" asked Lester.
"We don't know what happens in the end," said Luke.
"Please," said Laura.
"Story!" said the baby.

"Move over then," said Mrs. Large. She picked up the book and began to read: "'Watch where you're going, you silly Garbagetruck!' said Binky. Just then, Patty the Police Car came driving by . . . "

After a while, Mrs. Large stopped reading.

"What's that strange noise?" asked Lester.

"It's Mommy snoring," said Luke. "Daddy's snoring too."

"They must be very tired," said Laura, kindly.

"Shhhh!" said the baby.

The children crept from the sofa and got a blanket.

They covered Mr. and Mrs. Large and tucked them in.

"We'd better put ourselves to bed,"
   said Lester. "Come on."
"Should we take the food up with us?"
   asked Luke. "It *is* on trays."
"It's a pity to waste it," said Laura.
"I'm sure they wouldn't mind. Anyway,
   they wanted a quiet night in."
"Shhhh!" said the baby.

JILL MURPHY began writing and illustrating chidren's books when she was twenty-seven years old. Her first story about the ebullient Large family, *Five Minutes' Peace*, received the *Parents Magazine* Best Books for Babies Award, and was declared "painfully funny" by *The New York Times Book Review*. She is also the author of *The Worst Witch at Sea* and *Jeffrey Strangeways*, both novels for middle-grade readers; and *The Last Noo-Noo*, a picture book. She dedicates *A Quiet Night In*, the fourth Large family story, to exhausted parents everywhere. "This book is one from the heart," she says.